Y0-CAR-290

Sometimes
We Do

For further information, contact:
Tumblehome, Inc.
201 Newbury St, Suite 201
Boston, MA 02116
https://tumblehomebooks.org/

Library of Congress Control Number 2019903164
ISBN-13 978-1-943431-47-2
ISBN-10 1-943431-47-7

Moses, Omo
Sometimes We Do / Omo Moses – 1st ed
Illustrated by Diego Chaves

Printed in Taiwan
10 9 8 7 6 5 4 3 2 1

Tumblehome, Inc.

...And

Sometimes We Don't

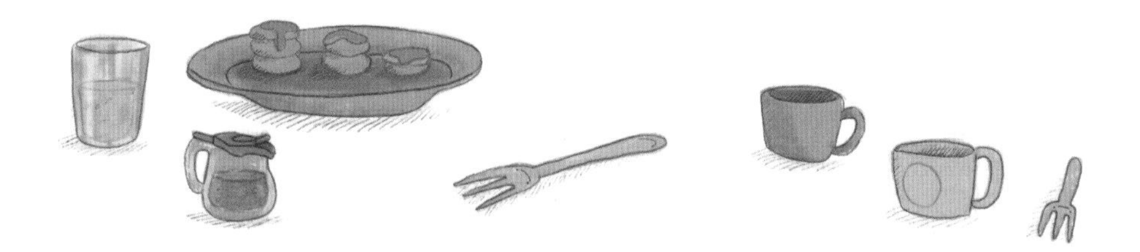

Written by Omo Moses
Illustrated by Diego Chaves

Some days are Daddy days, and some days are Mommy days.

On Daddy days we usually get up early and make a BIG breakfast!

Usually I ride trains while Daddy gets ingredients. Daddy says Grandma gave him a special ingredient that he puts in ALL of his pancakes.

"Two on the red car, three on the blue car, three in my belly, four on the last car, and one in my mouth."

"How many is that?" says Daddy.

"SO MANY!"

Sometimes I help Daddy make pancakes and sometimes I don't.
"Do you want BIG ones or small ones?" Daddy asks.
"One BIG one and lots of small ones."

"THICK ones or THIN ones?"
Daddy asks.
"THIN."
"More milk or more flour?"
FLOUR

"Mooooooooo."

"Are you a cow?" Daddy asks.

"Mooooooooo," I say.

Daddy says I'm hilarious.

Sometimes we make short stacks, sometimes we make TALL stacks.

Sometimes we make stacks as tall as trees.

Sometimes we count each pancake and sometimes we count stacks of pancakes.
"How many stacks you got?" Daddy says.
"One, two, three stacks of two, one stack of four and one stack of a hundred!"
"One hundred? That's ridiculous!"

"That's deeelicious! Mmm!"
"Mmmmmm, they're scrumptious!"
"Scrumptious? What's that?"
"Scrumptious is deeelicious."

"Do you know why Daddy's pancakes are so delicious?"
"Of course, Grandma gave you a special ingredient."
"Do you know what it is?"
"I don't, do you?"
"Of course," Daddy says, "You can always find it in Grandma's arms."
"In her arms?"
"And in her eyes and on her cheek," Daddy says.
"And in her pancakes?"
GRANDMA'S
SECRET
INGREDIENT

"Is it at the table?"
"It could be."
"Is it big or small?"
"Both."
"Hmmm. That's tricky.
Sweet or sour?"
"Sweet."
"Hard or soft?"
"Both."
"THAT'S ridiculous!"

"Daddy, are you sure Grandma's special ingredient is hard AND soft?"
"Yup," he says. "Hey! Look who rolled out of bed."
"Look who rolled out of bed!"

Sometimes Mommy and Kamara join us for breakfast.

"Look, Mommy. Now I have two stacks of three!"

"They're delicious," she says.

"They're SCRUMPTIOUS," I say.

"Chari have some?" says Kamara.

"You want more Kamara?"

"Here," I say.
"Oooooooh! NO FAIR!" she says.
"YES FAIR," I say.
"Kamara, Johari's sharing with you."
"Now what do I have, Mommy?"
"One plus three," Mommy says.
"Or?"
"Three plus one," Mommy says.
"FOUR MORE!" I say.
"THREE MORE,"
Kamara says.
"NO MORE," I say.
"YES MORE,"
says Kamara.
Usually I share my pancakes with mommy and Kamara...

But sometimes I don't!

"All done!" I say.
"All done?" Kamara asks.
"Zero stacks! And zero pieces!
Mmmm. Deeelicious!"
"All done?"
"Daddy, let's ride some trains!"

Sometimes we ride trains in the house.

"Not before you clean up," Mommy says.

"I WANT MORE PANCAKES," Kamara says.

"Don't worry, we can make more."

Usually we play ball before we ride some trains outside.

Usually we clean up.

AND SOMETIMES WE DON'T!
2

"So, Daddy."

"What's up?"

"I'm thinking of something hard AND soft AND sweet."

"That sounds tricky."

"It IS tricky."

"Sounds like Grandma's special ingredient?"

"Of course it's Grandma's special ingredient. Can I find it in your arms too?"

"I'm working on it."

"How's that?" Daddy asks.
"Good," I say.
The End...

Grandma's Pancake Recipe

2 cups flour ... 1 1/2 all purpose white
or half whole wheat and half white
2 tsp baking powder
1/4 tsp salt
1 tsp sugar
1/8th tsp of nutmeg

And a pinch of grandma's special ingredient...

1 1/2 to 2 cups milk
2 tablespoons of melted butter
A smidgen of butter or oil to grease the pan

1-2 eggs

1- Mix dry ingredients
2- Mix wet ingredients
3- Then add wet to dry
4- Turn the griddle to medium-low heat
5- Pour the pancake batter
6- Wait 2 minutes for bubbles, Flip it
7- Wait one minute until brown on other side

Add ins or ons:
Blueberries
Walnuts

Did you know that more math talk at mealtime means more math skills?

Learn More:

Can you find some of the "math" words that we used in the story in the pictures below? Try to use them in conversation with your child!

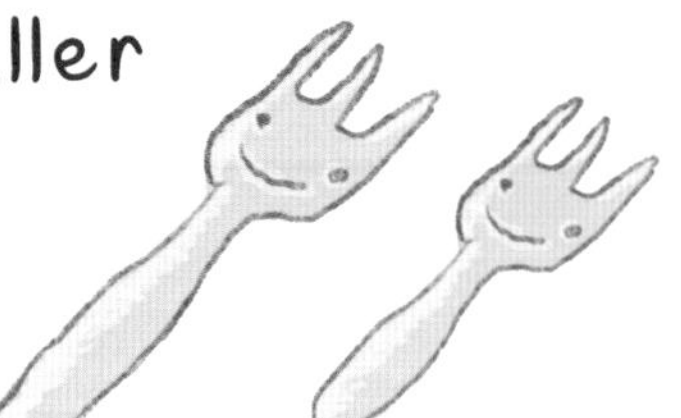

Round

Half

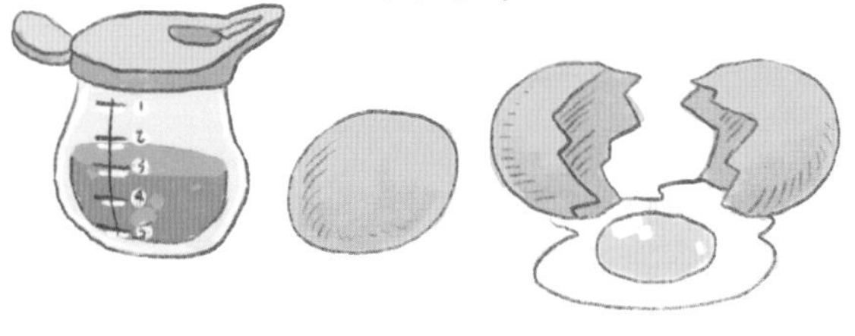

Fast

Empty

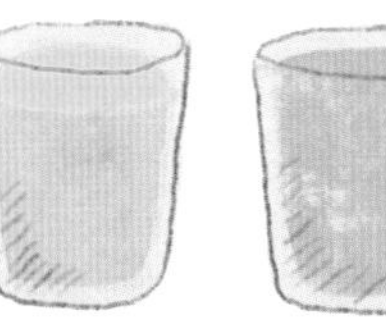